Franklin in the Dark

To Natalie and Gordon

Text © 1986 Contextx Inc.
Illustrations © 1986 Brenda Clark Illustrator Inc.

Kids Can Press gratefully acknowledges the financial support of the Government of Ontario; the Ontario Arts Council; the Canada Council for the Arts; and the Government of Canada, through the CBF, for our publishing activity.

Published in Canada and the U.S. by Kids Can Press Ltd.
25 Dockside Drive, Toronto, ON M5A 0B5

Kids Can Press is a Corus Entertainment Inc. company

www.kidscanpress.com

Book design by Michael Solomon and Brenda Clark

Printed and bound in Buji, Shenzhen, China, in 2/2019 by WKT Company

CM 86 20 19 18 17
CM 11 0 9 8 7 6 5 4 3 2 1
CDN PA 86 35 34 33 32 31 30
CMC PA 13 0 9 8 7 6 5

Library and Archives Canada Cataloguing in Publication

Bourgeois, Paulette
    Franklin in the dark / written by Paulette Bourgeois ; illustrated by Brenda Clark.

(A classic Franklin story)
ISBN 978-1-77138-007-2

    1. Franklin (Fictitious character : Bourgeois) — Juvenile fiction.
I. Clark, Brenda II. Title. III. Series: Classic Franklin story

PS8553.O85477F7 2013   jC813'.54   C2012-907883-2

Franklin in the Dark

Written by Paulette Bourgeois
Illustrated by Brenda Clark

Kids Can Press

FRANKLIN could slide down a riverbank all by himself. He could count forwards and backwards. He could even zip zippers and button buttons. But Franklin was afraid of small, dark places and that was a problem because …

Franklin was a turtle. He was afraid of crawling into his small, dark shell. And so, Franklin the turtle dragged his shell behind him.

Every night, Franklin's mother would take a flashlight and shine it into his shell.

"See," she would say, "there's nothing to be afraid of."

She always said that. She wasn't afraid of anything. But Franklin was sure that creepy things, slippery things, and monsters lived inside his small, dark shell.

So Franklin went looking for help. He walked until he met a duck.

"Excuse me, Duck. I'm afraid of small, dark places and I can't crawl inside my shell. Can you help me?"

"Maybe," quacked the duck. "You see, I'm afraid of very deep water. Sometimes, when nobody is watching, I wear my water wings. Would my water wings help you?"

"No," said Franklin. "I'm not afraid of water."

So Franklin walked and walked until he met a lion.

"Excuse me, Lion. I'm afraid of small, dark places and I can't crawl inside my shell. Can you help me?"

"Maybe," roared the lion. "You see, I'm afraid of great, loud noises. Sometimes, when nobody is looking, I wear my earmuffs. Would my earmuffs help you?"

"No," said Franklin. "I'm not afraid of great, loud noises."

So Franklin walked and walked and walked
until he met a bird.

"Excuse me, Bird. I'm afraid of small, dark
places and I can't crawl inside my shell. Can you
help me?"

"Maybe," chirped the bird. "I'm afraid of flying
so high that I get dizzy and fall to the ground.
Sometimes, when nobody is looking, I pull my
parachute. Would my parachute help you?"

"No," said Franklin. "I'm not afraid of flying
high and getting dizzy."

So Franklin walked and walked and walked and walked until he met a polar bear.

"Excuse me, Polar Bear. I'm afraid of small, dark places and I can't crawl inside my shell. Can you help me?"

"Maybe," growled the bear. "You see, I'm afraid of freezing on icy, cold nights. Sometimes, when nobody is looking, I wear my snowsuit to bed. Would my snowsuit help you?"

"No," said Franklin. "I'm not afraid of freezing on icy, cold nights."

Franklin was tired and hungry. He walked and walked and walked until he met his mother.

"Oh, Franklin. I was so afraid you were lost."

"You were afraid? I didn't know mothers were ever afraid," said Franklin.

"Well, did you find some help?" she asked.

"No. I met a duck who was afraid of deep water."

"Hmmm," she said.

"Then I met a lion who was afraid of great, loud noises."

"Uh, hmmmm," she said.

"And then I met a bird who was afraid of
falling and a polar bear who was afraid of freezing."
"Oh," she said. "They were all afraid of
something."
"Hmmmm," said Franklin.

It was getting late. Franklin was very tired and very hungry. They walked and walked until they were home.

Franklin's mother gave him a cold supper and a warm hug. And then she sent him off to bed. "Good night, dear," she said.

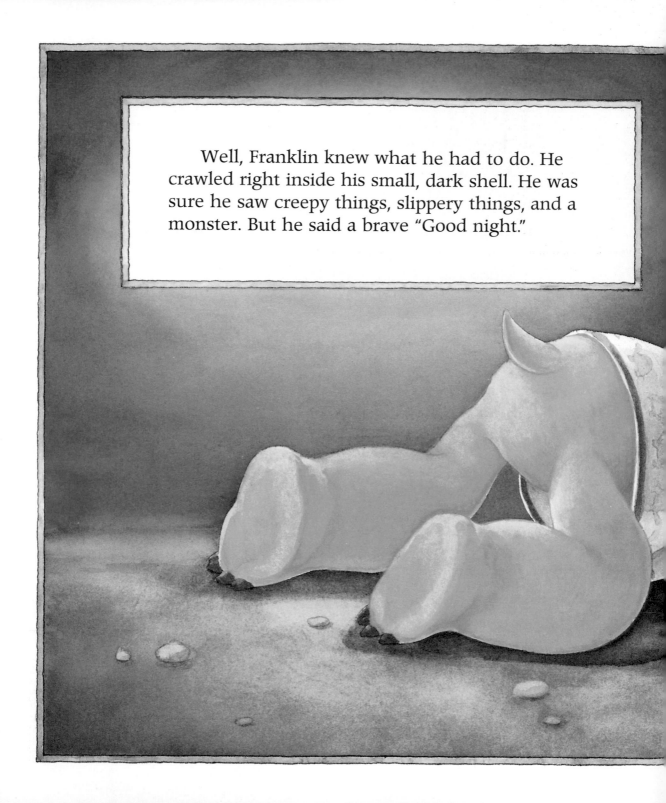

Well, Franklin knew what he had to do. He crawled right inside his small, dark shell. He was sure he saw creepy things, slippery things, and a monster. But he said a brave "Good night."

And then, when nobody was looking, Franklin the turtle turned on his night light.